Because a Little Bug Went Ka- CHOO!

By
Rosetta Stone

Illustrated by
Michael Frith

BEGINNER BOOKS
A Division of Random House, Inc.

ER
F
STONE. R
BECA

You may not believe it,
but here's how it happened.

One fine summer morning . . .

. . . a little bug sneezed.

Because of that sneeze,
a little seed dropped.

Because that seed dropped,
a worm got hit.

Because he got hit,
that worm got mad.

Because he got mad,
he kicked a tree.

Because of that kick,

a coconut dropped.

Because
that nut
dropped,
a turtle
got bopped.

Because he got bopped,
that turtle named Jake
fell on his back
with a splash
in the lake.

Because of that splash,
a hen got wet.

Because she got wet,
that hen got mad.

Because she got mad,
that hen kicked a bucket.

Because of that kick,
the bucket went up.

Because it went up . . .

. . . the bucket
came down.

Because it came down,
it hit Farmer Brown.

And
that
bucket
got
stuck
on
his
head.

Because it got stuck,
Farmer Brown
phoned for help.

Because of his phone call,
policemen came speeding.

Because they were speeding,
they hit a big stone.

And so one policeman
flew up all alone.

Because he flew up . . .

. . . he
had
to
come
down.

And because he came down
on the boat Mary Lou . . .
and because he hit hard . . .

he went right on through.

He made a big hole
in the boat Mary Lou.

Because of that hole,
the boat started to sink.
And because it was sinking . . .
well, what do you think?

Everyone, EVERYONE started to yelp.

And Mrs. Brown called
on the phone for more help.

Because of her phone call,
MORE help came . . . FAST!

They tied a strong rope
to the Mary Lou's mast.

And because of that rope
the boat didn't go down.
But it had to be fixed.
So they started for town.

And because
they went THERE—
it's true, I'm afraid—
they ran right into
a circus parade.

And THAT started something
they'll never forget.

And as far as I know
it is going on yet.

And that's how it happened.
Believe me. It's true.
Because . . .
just because . . .
a small bug
went KA-CHOO!

Rosetta Stone

...is a multi-faceted personality whose multiple careers have covered most of the media and much of the globe. This is, however, Rosetta's first book for children ...at least, under this particular name.

Michael Frith

...has been involved in a very large number of books for children, both as an editor-art director and as an author-illustrator. He has had both the latter functions in the Beginner Books *My Amazing Book of Autographs* and *Some of Us Walk, Some Fly, Some Swim,* and he wrote the Bright and Early Book *I'll Teach My Dog 100 Words.*

Mr. Frith describes himself as a "crypto-Bermudian." He and his family now live in New York.